The Little Tuatara

National Library of New Zealand Cataloguing-in-Publication Data

Cunningham, Robin.
The little tuatara / Robin Cunningham.
ISBN - 13: 978-1-86950-544-8
[1. Tuatara fiction. 2. Petrels fiction. 3. Sea birds fiction.
4. Dinosaurs fiction.] I. Title.
NZ823.2 dc 22

First published 2005
Reprinted 2005, 2007 (twice)
HarpercollinsPublishers (New Zealand) Limited
P.O. Box 1, Auckland

ISBN - 13: 978 1 86950 544 8
ISBN - 10: 1 86950 544 1

Designed by Worksight
Printed by Everbest Printing, China

The Little Tuatara

written by Robin Cunningham

Illustrated by Samer Usama Hatam

The island where the little tuatara lived was far, far away from the rest of the world. It was just a small green speck adrift in a great blue ocean.

Ever since he had hatched,
the little tuatara had been lonely.

Sea birds lived on the island too, mostly petrels, but they spent their time riding the wind watching with their sharp eyes for fish in the sea below.

One day the little tuatara moved into a new burrow. It was deep and snug and well protected from the cutting winds that swept the island.

He was drifting off to sleep in the comfortable darkness when there was a swoosh and a scuffling feathery sound in the entrance of the burrow.

Suddenly the little tuatara found himself nose to nose with a petrel.

'Go away,' said the little tuatara.
'Get out of my burrow!'

The petrel squawked and fluffed out his feathers until he looked like an enormous blue and white tea-cosy.

He glared at the little tuatara, his wicked eyes glinting in the darkness.

'This is my burrow,' hissed the petrel.
'I made it!'

'I'm so sorry,' said the little tuatara,
'but I thought it was empty.'

'Well it's not,' snapped the petrel.
'I go off on a fishing trip and come home
to find a lizard in my burrow.'

The little tuatara's scaly peaks stood up stiffly, like sails on a toy boat.

'I'm not a lizard! I'm a tuatara!'

'Really?' The petrel was very surprised. 'I've heard of tuatara. There aren't many of your kind left, are there?'

'I don't know,' said the little tuatara. 'I've never met many.'

The petrel unfluffed his feathers with a soft swooshing sound and studied the little tuatara.

'Well, I've been around and I know lots of things. You, my friend, are very rare.'

'What does that mean?'

'It means that there aren't very many tuatara left.'

'Look,' the petrel said kindly, 'why don't you stay and share my burrow? I'm a day creature and you're a night creature. We won't get in each other's way.'

So the petrel and the little tuatara settled down in the burrow together.

They became very good friends and the petrel told the little tuatara stories of the places he'd been and the things he'd seen.

The story the little tuatara liked best of all was about the dinosaurs, his ancient relatives; and this is the story . . .

Long, long ago when the world was young
and full of fire and fury, the earth was ruled by
dinosaurs. They were strange and exotic creatures.

Triceratops and stegosaurus,
Pterodactyl and brontosaurus,

Protoceratops and allosaurus,
Iguanodon and tyrannosaurus,

And *Rhynchocephalia triassic,*
The tuatara.

They were mean, lean
Biters and fighters,

Crunchers and munchers,
Roarers and clawers,

Savagers and ravagers,
Those terrible creatures,
The dinosaurs.

They were ferocious
and atrocious,
Scaleful and baleful,
Snappers and trappers,
Stompers and trompers,

Those terrible creatures
Thundering over the
face of the earth.

And then, as the world grew older, the dinosaurs began to die. But the tiniest of the dinosaurs didn't die — somehow they survived. And they are the tuatara, the last of the dinosaurs.

The little tuatara
would sigh when
the petrel finished
the story.
'Fancy that,' he
would say.
'Fancy me being
so special.'

'oh yes indeed, you are very special,' the petrel would say. 'In fact, you are so special that people have made laws to protect you. No one is allowed to hurt you. I'm very proud to share my burrow with you.'

Now the little tuatara is no longer lonely. He sits quietly in his burrow dreaming of those days so long ago when his ancient relatives ruled the earth.

And if I'm not mistaken, he'll
be there for a long, long time.

The tuatara is found on about 20 islands off the shores of New Zealand.

The Maori word 'tuatara' means 'peaks on the back'.

The tuatara often shares burrows with petrels and other sea birds.

Tuatara are coloured black-brown to a dull green; sometimes they are spotted with a yellowish colour.

They have scales on their body.

The tuatara has five toes on each of its feet and each of those toes has a sharp claw.

The tuatara eats moths, crickets and beetles.

Tuatara eggs take from about 13 to 15 months to hatch.

The tuatara is nocturnal. That means it hunts for food at night.

However tuatara do sometimes like to sunbathe on a warm rock.

The tuatara lives for a long time — 100 to 300 years!